Henry Hyena, Why Won't You Laugh?

Written By
Doug Jantzen

Illustrated by Jean Claude

ALADDIN

New York   London   Toronto   Sydney   New Delhi

ALADDIN

An imprint of Simon & Schuster Children's Publishing Division
1230 Avenue of the Americas, New York, New York 10020
First Aladdin hardcover edition July 2015
Text copyright © 2015 by Doug Jantzen
Illustrations copyright © 2015 by Jean Claude
For information about special discounts for bulk purchases, please contact
Simon & Schuster Special Sales at 1-866-506-1949 or business@simonandschuster.com.
The Simon & Schuster Speakers Bureau can bring authors to your live event. For more information or
to book an event contact the Simon & Schuster Speakers Bureau at 1-866-248-3049 or
visit our website at www.simonspeakers.com.
Designed by Karina Granda
The illustrations for this book were rendered digitally.
The text of this book was set in Archer.
Manufactured in China 0515 SCP
2 4 6 8 10 9 7 5 3 1
Library of Congress Cataloging-in-Publication Data
Jantzen, Douglas.
Henry Hyena, why won't you laugh? / Douglas Jantzen ; illustrated by Jean Claude. —
First Aladdin hardcover edition.
pages cm
Summary: "Young Henry Hyena loves to join his fellow hyenas in poking fun at animals at the zoo.
But the jokes aren't making Henry laugh anymore—with the help of a wise old giraffe,
Henry gets his laugh back in an unexpectedway"— Provided by publisher.
[1. Stories in rhyme. 2. Laughter—Fiction. 3. Hyenas—Fiction. 4. Zoos—Fiction.]
I. Claude, Jean, illustrator. II. Title.
PZ8.3.J266Hen 2015
[E]—dc23
2014040724 ISBN 978-1-4814-2822-4 (hc)
ISBN 978-1-4814-2823-1 (eBook)

To my wife and best friend, Nancy,
without you this would never have been possible, and
to my daughters and biggest fans, Jadeyn and Avery,
for always finding new ways to make me laugh.
—D. J.

To my family—Ben, Lucy, Miranda, and Martin.
All the love in the world.
—J. C.

A funny thing happened
today at the zoo.
Young Henry Hyena
began to feel blue.

Now this kind of thing
is really quite rare
for hyenas always
laugh without care.

They **laugh** at the monkeys
who swing from the trees.

They **laugh** at the storks
and their wobbly knees.

They **giggle** whenever a bird says, "chirp."
They roar when they hear an elephant **burp**.

Hyenas just laugh because that's what they do.
They laugh at anyone who lives at the zoo.

But not young Henry.
At least not today.
His friends couldn't even
get him to play.

do not
disturb

He didn't join in while they **teased** a few bears.

He chose not to help when they **chased** several hares.

He wouldn't cut holes in the llamas' new socks,
or knock down a lion cub's tower of blocks.

No matter the prank,
Henry just wouldn't laugh.

It was time to seek help from
a wise old giraffe.

Now as soon as a problem
arose at the zoo,
Dr. Long was the one
who knew what to do.

He gave speaking lessons
to several shy parrots.

He worked with a rabbit
who wouldn't eat carrots.

Why just this past week
he sat in the sun
and coached a cheetah
who hated to run.

"Dr. Long," Henry said,
"my **giggle is gone**."

I can't seem to laugh.
I don't know what's wrong!

Like, today when a goat tripped on a limb,
rather than laugh, I felt sorry for him.

And later when the zebra let out a yelp,
instead of chuckling, I offered to help.

Oh Dr. Long, you must think me a fool.
I failed to laugh at a hiccupping mule."

"Henry, my boy," said the wise old giraffe.
"Let me explain why it is you won't laugh.

It's not that you're sick, and you're far from a fool.
You've just learned that **laughing at others is cruel**.

I'm proud of you, Henry,
so cheer up and grin.
Your laugh will come out
when the kind deeds begin."

Henry's face brightened and
his smile soon returned,
then back home he raced
to explain what he learned.

His friends gathered 'round and soon all agreed
that Henry Hyena was quite right indeed.

So off they all went to try something new—
to become the nicest ones at the zoo.

They **brought** honey muffins
to each of the bears,

then **joined** all the lions
for musical chairs.

They **sang** with the birds and **read** to the boars.

They **helped** as the monkeys completed their chores.

They even **jumped rope** with
the storks and the crocs,

and **knitted** the llamas some new pairs of socks.

They did all these things and saw right away . . .
being nice was really the best way to play.

Young Henry joined in and smiled with delight
as all of the animals joked through the night.

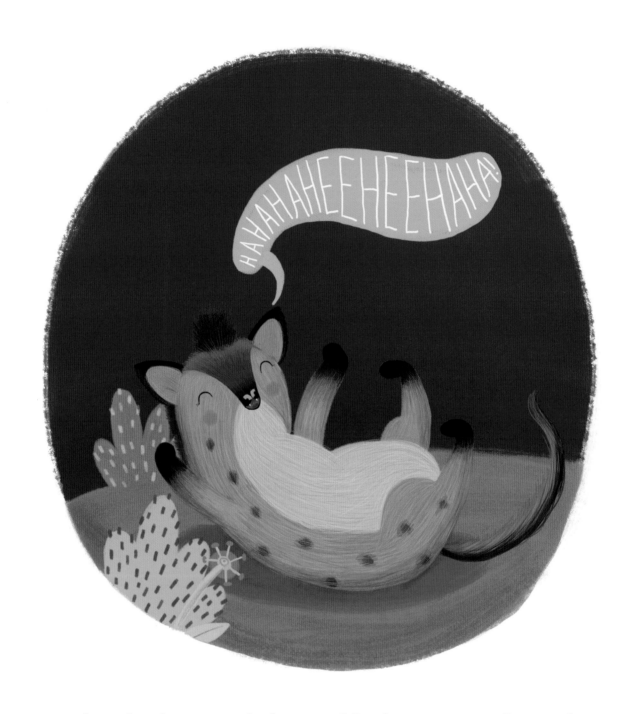

They had so much fun and before it was through,
**Henry's laugh was the
loudest of all at the zoo**.